EAT AT JOE'S

CHIEF

First published in 1976
This edition published by HarperCollins Publishers Ltd in 2001

3 5 7 9 10 8 6 4

ISBN: 0 00 711151 7

Copyright © 1976 Richard Scarry Corporation
A CIP catalogue record for this title is available from the British Library

The HarperCollins website address is: www.fireandwater.com

Printed in Thailand

Richard Scarry
Busiest People Ever

Collins

An imprint of HarperCollinsPublishers

The busy people are on their way to work.
Bre-e-e-e-t! Sergeant Murphy blows his whistle to stop
the traffic and let the workers cross the street.

Bre-e-e-t! Lowly Worm and Huckle Cat are helping
Sergeant Murphy direct traffic. Lowly and Huckle want
to be policemen when they grow up.

Miney and Moe, the television
camera bugs, take pictures of things
that happen in Busytown. The pictures
will be part of a television programme.

clergyman

TELEVISIONS BOOKS

bookseller

SPECTACLES

optician

SPORTS

SPORT SHOP

Sergeant Murphy rides around town to make sure that everything is peaceful. If the chief of police hears of any trouble, he tells Sergeant Murphy about it over the radio.

"Sergeant Murphy! Sergeant Murphy!"
The police station is calling Murphy on the radio.
"Grocer Cat has just telephoned. His grocery store has been robbed!"

"Quickly! We must try to catch the thief!"
says Sergeant Murphy.

road painter

ditch digger

SHOEMAKER

Get off that fresh cement, Mr. Frumble!

FRESH CEMENT

radio operator

POLICE STATION

DELICATESSEN

CONFECTIONERY

chief of police

RX

CHEMIST

HARDWARE

HATS

chemist

FLOWERS

ICE CREAM

ice cream man

EAT HATS

sandwich-board man

ELECTRIC SUPPLIES

GROCERIES

BANANAS

APPLES

ORANGES

flower seller

TV

Grocer Cat

Sergeant Murphy speeds
through the street on his
motor-cycle.
"Faster, faster!" says Lowly.
"We must catch the thief."

postman

fireman

cleansing worker

Stop thief.

miner

rug salesman

violinist

TV repairman

bugdozer driver

drummer

building worker

football player

locksmith

golfer

brush salesman

magician

florist

"Look!" says Sergeant Murphy. "The thief must be in that crowd of people. All of them are carrying things. How can we tell which one stole something from Grocer Cat's store?"

Lowly looks at the crowd and suddenly shouts, "There's the thief!"

Lowly chases after the thief and tackles him around the legs. Who can it be?

billboard paster

juggler

architect

life-guard

street cleaner

lawyer

sailor

banana eater

bass fiddler

plumber

soldier

carpenter

tennis player

window cleaner

another tennis player

It's Bananas Gorilla! And Lowly has caught him.
"But how did you know Bananas was the thief?"
asks Sergeant Murphy.

"Well," says Lowly, "out of all those people
Bananas was the only one carrying something that
could be stolen from a grocery store."

Very good thinking, Policeman Lowly.
Take Bananas off to jail now.

A Visit to the Big City

Mother Cat is taking Huckle and Lowly to the city.
What do you think they are going to do there?
They have to take the train. Mother Cat
sits in the passenger coach. Huckle and Lowly
sit with the driver of the engine.
To-o-o-o-t! Lowly pulls the whistle.
Off they go.

bulb changer

taxi driver

travelling salesman

skier

mountain climber

scouts

scout leader

porter

cook

waiter

signalman

Mother C

passengers

DINING CAR

COACH

wheel tapper

BUSYTOWN

TICKETS

TIME TABLE

NEWSPAPERS

BAGGAGE

ticket seller

newsdealer

baggage
checker

fork-lift
truck
operator

snack-cart
attendant

sandwich eater

station master

conductor

oiler

truck driver

bricklayer

mechanical
shovel

plumber carpenters

bulldozer operator

plumber

bricklayer

HOUSES
FOR
SALE

mortar mixer

bathtub
deliverymen

driver

newspaper reader

carpenters

electrician

roofer

painter

paper-hanger

gardener

SOLD

nail
spiller

stove and refrigerator
deliveryman

TV

The train chugs along the tracks
on the way to the big city.
Suddenly Lowly shouts, "STOP!
Something is wrong!"
The train stops.
Lowly jumps down from the locomotive
and runs to the switch.
What can the matter be?

driver

school-bus driver

SCHOOL BUS

log cutter

log hauler

tree chopper

kite flier

vagrant

grass mower

A goods train is speeding towards them
on the same line.
Lowly moves the switch . . . just in time!
The goods train rolls onto another line.
Lowly has saved everyone from a terrible accident.
Lowly is certainly a good railway worker, isn't he?

*Watch out,
Mr. Frumble!*

ICE
CREAM

TRAVEL GIFT SHOP LEFT LUGGAGE FLOWERS

FLY

COME
TO
LAND

MAIL

luggage trolley driver

sleeping-car

workers running
to catch their train

sweeper

PLATFORM 3

PLATFORM 2

PLATFORM 1

SNACK BAR

NEWSAGENT

window
cleaner

clock fixer

TV

TICKETS

TIMETABLE

EXIT

jewellery
seller

TO TAXIS

porter

pencil
seller

Finally the train arrives
at the city's railway station.
What a big, busy place it is!
Look! Someone is there to greet
the three arrivals. Who can he be?

steel workers

nosy pedestrian

welder

crane operator

cement mixer

foreman

NOW BUILDING A NEW SKYSCRAPER

TV1

A television producer has come to meet them. A few days ago he had invited Huckle and Lowly to appear on his television show.

He drives them through the city streets to the television studio.

CONTROL ROOM

musicians

cameraman

TV 1

TV1

TAXI

doorman

In the television studio,
Huckle and Lowly sing a jolly song.
People all over the country can see
and hear the programme on their
television sets.

When Huck and Lowly return to Busytown,
all their friends will tell them that they
saw the programme, too.

Grandma Cat lives far away, but she sees
Huckle and Lowly on her television set.
She is very surprised and pleased.
"I must visit my two television entertainers
soon," she says.
Would YOU like to be a television singer, too?

Mr. Frumble's Bad Day

Mr. Frumble is going to work.
He forgot to open the garage doors
before he backed the car.
What a bad way to start the day!

butcher

manager

cashier

There are a few things
Mr. Frumble must do on his way
to work. First, he stops to shop
at the supermarket. Look at
what he's done now!

book borrowers

librarian

Next, he goes to the library to borrow a book.
The librarian does not like noisy sneezers.

barber

At the barber shop he fidgets so much that
the barber cuts his tie by mistake.

chemist

Mr. Frumble has a little accident when he
buys some vitamins from the chemist.

Then he tries on a suit at the clothing store.
"I think you need a larger size, Mr. Frumble."

He tries on a hat.
"Don't pull it down so hard, Mr. Frumble."

laundrette attendant

He washes his laundry at the laundromat.
"I think you have put too much soap in the
machine, Mr. Frumble."

nurse

At Dr. Lion's office he breaks the scales.
Does Mr. Frumble weigh THAT much?

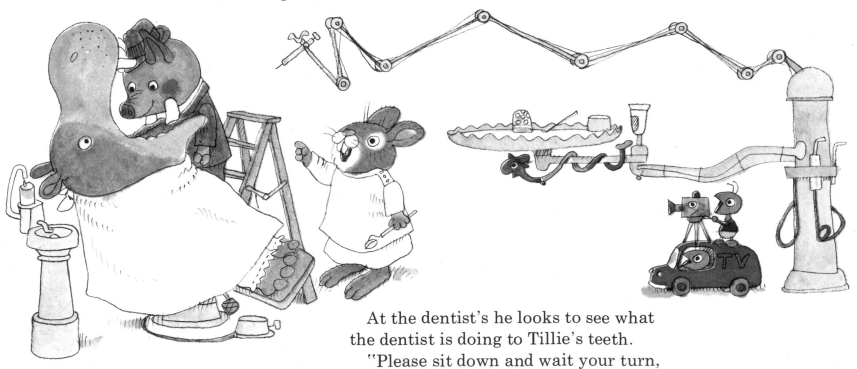

At the dentist's he looks to see what
the dentist is doing to Tillie's teeth.
"Please sit down and wait your turn,
Mr. Frumble."

waitress

chef

waiter

Mr. Frumble goes into a restaurant to eat his lunch.
He sees the chef cooking some Flambéed Bananas.

Mr. Frumble thinks the fire is dangerous.
He throws water on it.

The chef is furious.
"I NEED fire to cook my Bananas,"
he says. "Now you have ruined them."

The angry chef frightens Mr. Frumble.
He runs out of the restaurant.
Oops! Watch where you are going, Mr. Frumble.

DRIVE-IN BANK

SCHOOL

teacher   pupils

POST OFFICE

post-office clerk

bank
teller

Bananamobile driver

Mr. Frumble gets back into his car, but
again he doesn't look where he is going.
He runs into a water hydrant and
accidentally puts out another fire
on the chef's Flaming Bananas.

THE DAILY EAGLE

typist

editor

newsboy

photographer

reporter

MUSIC SHOP

RESTAURANT

chimney
sweep

OUR SPECIALITY—
FLAMBÉED BANANAS

AUTOMOBILES

BICYCLES

THE
COFFEE
POT

COFFEE

car salesman

newspaper
deliveryman

NEWSPAPER
DELIVERY

linotype operator

printers

bulldozer operator

bugdozer operator

road layer

dump-truck driver

PETROL

Mr. Frumble!
How did you ever get your car on that new road?
It's not ready yet for drivers. The workers are
still busy building it.
Get off immediately.
You have certainly had a bad day, haven't you,
Mr. Frumble?

pumpkin-car driver

petrol pump attendant

car greaser

road-roller operator

dump-truck driver

"It's about time you went home," Lowly tells Mr. Frumble, "before you cause any more trouble. I will call a breakdown truck for you."

SOS

pilot

breakdown truck driver

A breakdown truck comes and takes Mr. Frumble home.

So long, Mr. Frumble. You didn't even get to work today. Maybe things will be better tomorrow.

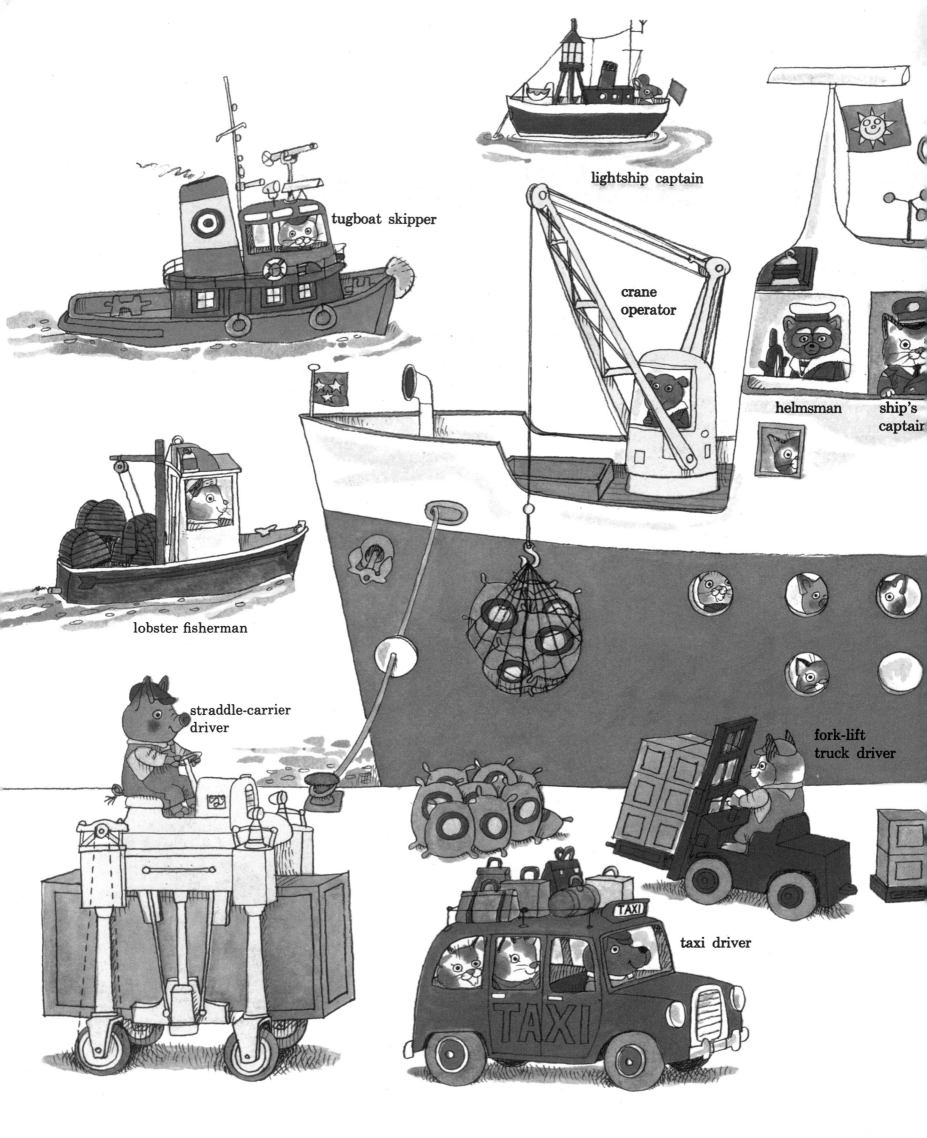

lightship captain

tugboat skipper

crane
operator

helmsman

ship's
captain

lobster fisherman

straddle-carrier
driver

fork-lift
truck driver

taxi driver

TAXI

TAXI

Down by the Busy Sea

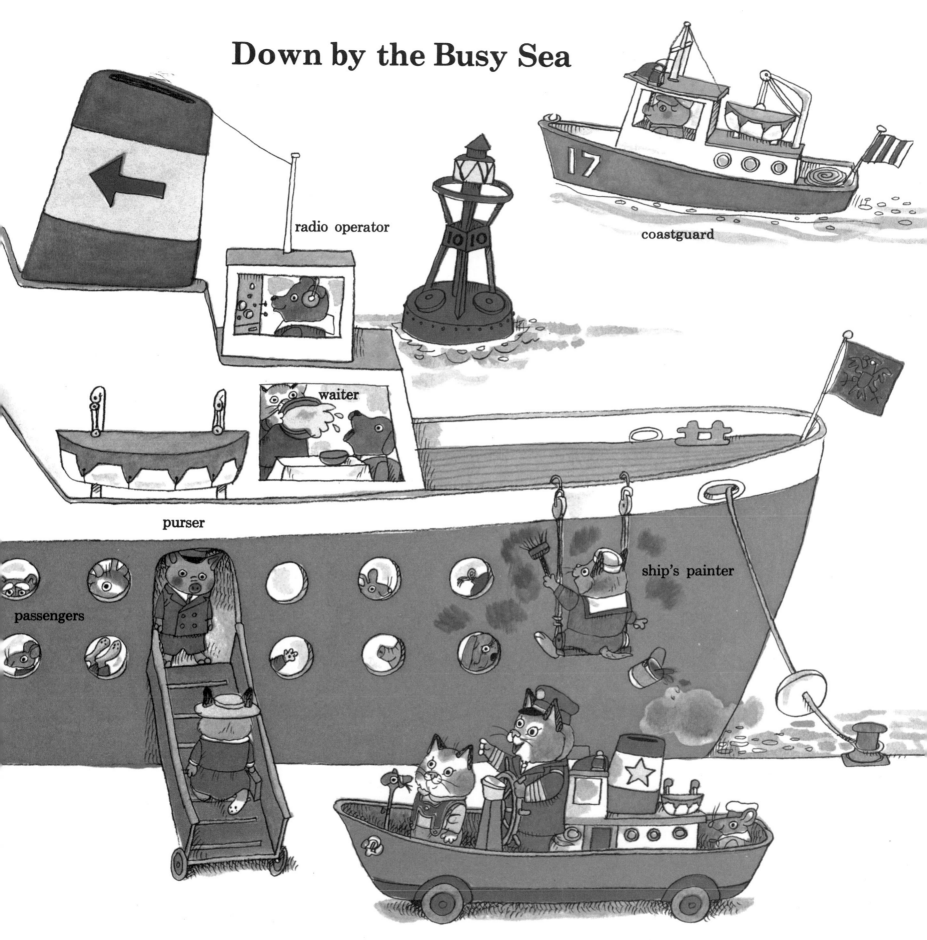

radio operator

coastguard

waiter

purser

passengers

ship's painter

Huckle and Lowly are visiting Captain Salty down at the pier.
The captain shows them all the things there are to see at a harbour.
"This is a passenger ship," he explains. "It will carry people
across the ocean to visit their friends in distant places."
Lowly thinks *he* would like to be a sea captain when he grows up.

lighthouse keeper

sailor

fishermen

Next, Captain Salty points to a cargo ship.
"It can carry all kinds of things to distant ports,"
he says. "Just now cars are being loaded into its hold.
The ship will carry them across the sea, and people in
far-away countries will drive them."
"LOOK!" cries Captain Salty loudly.
"There is a fire on that barge. We must help!
Hop onto the fire-tender. Let's go!"

captain

stevedores

fire-tender
captain

fork-lift
truck driver

harbour
police

giant-crane
operator

dockside train driver

submarine skipper

Mr. Frumble,
the boat wrecker

The fire-tender rushes
towards the burning barge
and sprays it with water.

ferry-boat captain

FERRY

fire-tender firemen

lazy fisherman

Captain Tillie has jumped off the burning barge.
"Help! Help!" she cries.
Lowly jumps overboard with a life-belt to save
her.

A wet Captain Tillie thanks Lowly
and gives him a big kiss. Isn't it
amazing that such a little fellow
can rescue such a big sea captain?
Good work, Sea Captain Lowly.

hay baler

tractor driver

cabbage picker

grass mower

farm hand

woodcutter

poster-paster

CHEW

wall builder

hay lifter

fence builder

Grandma Cat comes to Visit

Grandma Cat is coming to visit the Cat family.
The whole family drives to the airport to meet her.

As the car passes Farmer Goat's farm, Lowly asks,
"Can we stop and buy some apples?"

Father Cat says, "No. We don't want to be late
arriving at the airport."

surveyor

windmill fixer

apple picker

lightning rod installer

apple gatherer

apple-sauce cooker

corn picker

APPLES

apple seller

water pumper

pumpkin seller

apple eater

glider pilot

helicopter pilot

air-traffic controller

radar controller

weatherman

ground controller

They arrive at the airport ahead of time.
While they wait for Grandma's plane to come in,
Lowly visits the flight compartment of a plane
that will soon take off. Now he would like to be
an aeroplane pilot instead of a sea captain.
Huckle visits the airport control tower.
He would like to be an air-traffic controller
and tell the planes when to land and take off.
What would YOU like to do at an airport?

pilot

LOUNGE

co-pilot

flight engineer

pilot

flight attendant

BUSYTOWN AIRPORT

TO ALL FLIGHTS

CHECK-IN COUNTER

TAXI

Mr. Frumble, the
upside-down pilot

parachutist

balloonist

aeroplane washer

FOLLOW
ME

SWISSAIR

stewardess

fuel man

postman

AIRMAIL
POST OFFICE

luggage porter

FUEL

Here comes Grandma's plane now.
But why is she traveling on a big cargo plane?
Why isn't she on a passenger plane?

*Mr. Frumble!
You're washing
the wrong plane!*

food-delivery
person

Well! It seems that Grandma was bringing
so many apples with her that she had to come
on a cargo plane. Grandma plans to make lots
of apple pies during her visit.

"Hi, Grandma. It's good to see you,"
says Huckle.

"And all your apples, too," says Lowly.

Busy House Workers

Grandma is happy to be visiting so many busy workers.

Lowly works hard to make his bed.

Huckle works to tidy his room.

Little Sister empties a wastebasket.

Daddy washes the dirty dishes.

Mummy cooks the meals for the family.

And Grandma and Lowly work hard making lots of apple pies to eat. Lowly is especially good at peeling apples.

While the apple pies are baking in the oven,
they all watch the television news of the week.

They see Lowly,
the policeman, capturing
Bananas Gorilla.

They see Lowly,
the railway worker,
saving the train.

They see Huckle and Lowly
singing on television.

They see Lowly,
the sea captain,
saving Captain Tillie.

After seeing all those jobs, Lowly, what would you
like best of all to be when you grow up?
"Why," says Lowly, "I think best of all I would
like to be an apple-pie eater."
Well, Lowly, I think that is very nice work indeed.

Would YOU like to help Lowly eat apple pies?

Have you read these other books about the busy world of Richard Scarry?